The BLUE and the GRAY

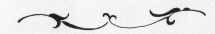

The BLUE
and the GRAY

BY *Eve Bunting*

ILLUSTRATED BY *Ned Bittinger*

SCHOLASTIC PRESS
New York

My dad and I and J.J. Huff, my friend,
stand here in what will be our house
when it is done.

Three doors from us is J.J.'s house.

It's great he'll be
that close to me.

Above us workmen hammer nails
and talk of baseball games they've seen.

Tall ladders lean
against the houses,
cross between,
like catwalks.

The three of us look out across the field
all hillocky and hummocky
with tufted grass and stubby flowers,
white as new sprinkled snow,
the kind that grow
wherever grass can grow.
The field will stay the way it is,
for now.

"But long ago,"
my father says,
"it wasn't always so."

In 1862 this was a battleground,
and here two armies fought
and soaked the grass with blood.
I guess the flowers were red instead of white that night.

It was the Civil War,
the North against the South,
the blue against the gray.
White against black.
White against white.
Us against us,
to tell it right.
My dad says that's the saddest kind of war there is,
though every war is sad
and most are bad.

Behind us there's a mound of wet cement
and lumpy bags of Ready-Mix.

High up
a workman on a ladder scrapes the wall
and pats it smooth
as frosting on a cake.
He's careful
round the porthole windows
Mother wants.

"We'll have a view," she'd said
and lifted me
so I could see the oak tree
and the mountains.

"Let's walk across the field,"
my father says.
"You see that grassy hump?
That's where the Rebels and their horses hid,
and in the orchard, just beyond."

My father knows the history of this place,
and he tells us that we must
remember and revere.
I didn't understand the word
but he explained.
It means that we must honor all that happened here.

We talk about it as we walk.
I wonder if the Rebels said their prayers
before they crossed this open field?
And if the Union soldiers knew
that they'd die too,
the gray beside the blue?

For in the end, my father says,
this was a field of bones.

Our dog is racing here today
chasing a blur of birds
that lift and circle over him,
then land again
beyond his reach.
They fluff their feathers
while he stumps and barks.
Each bark is sharp enough to be a shot.
But it is not.

It was back then.

On this wide field two armies met.
We won't forget.

Their red flags tossed and flamed like fire.
The barrels of their muskets
hard and black
gave back
the dazzle of the sun.

And on the ridge
behind where we are now
the Northern general stood.
In days before the war began
the Southern captain was his friend.

But then he waited on that lonely ridge
for friendship's end.

"Those two were friends before the war?"
J.J. moves closer still to me.
"It could have been brother against brother."

"Sometimes it was," my father says.

"We'd never!" J.J. looks at me.
"We'd never!" I agree.

The little puffs of smoke
burst like gray dust
around the barrel of each rifle gun,
floated behind them as they'd run
man after man.

Hard from the ridge
the Yankee guns replied.
And soldiers died.

Back at the house
there is the slam
of wooden plank on wooden post.
Our air is filled with sawdust
and the smell of newness.

The high-up workman shinnies down
and gets a can of Coke.
He takes his cap off,
hand thick crusted with cement.
"We're getting there," he says.
"Soon you'll be moving in."

We grin.

He looks across the field.
"Nice here, nice view.
It will be quiet, too,
when we have gone."

It wasn't then.

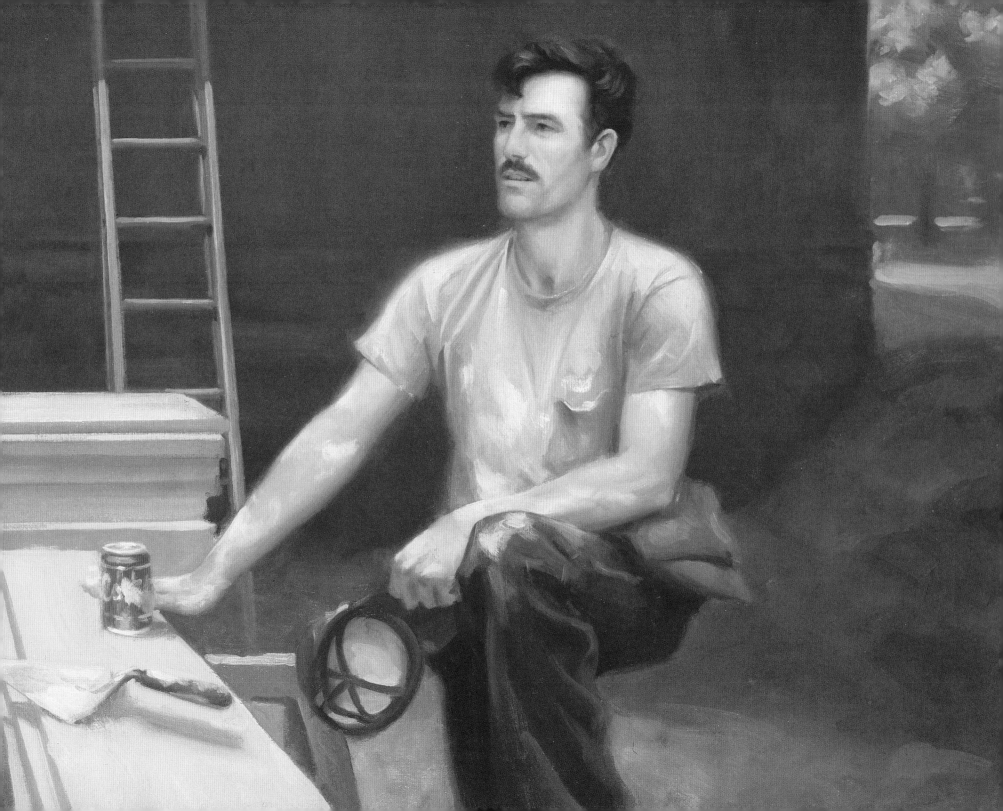

The Rebels almost reached the ridge
before the Yankee cannons opened up,
burst in a cloud of fire and smoke
that rose above the trees,
ripped legs and arms away.
The flag had fallen in the dirt.
Another soldier snatched it up.

And still they came
through buckshot, bullets, cannon shell.
They came
and fell.

Some ran for cover.
Others lay, like washing
tossed upon the grass to dry.
Some held their handkerchiefs above their heads
to show surrender.
And their moans and cries
were carried on the battlesmoke to heaven.

I think the angels wept.

"Was it as hard a war as Desert Storm?
My father fought in that."
J.J. looks closely at my dad.

"As hard," my father says.
"Hundreds of men were lost that day.
They say
the carts that took away the wounded
stretched for miles along the road."

We turn to look.

There's nothing on the road
but passing cars,
a yellow moving van,
the workers' trucks, parked on the side.
We turn again to stare across the field
though there are only birds to see.
Our dog has gone,
moved on to look for dumber birds.

"It isn't fair," J.J. exclaims.
"There ought to be a marker here."

My father nods.
"There ought to be.
So many battlegrounds have disappeared
without a name.
This one's the same.
There'll be no marker here."

"Except our homes," I say.
"And all the other homes."

"And all those days,"
J.J. agrees,
"when we play football on the field
and sled when there is snow.
And we will know
the way it was.
And we'll remember."

"*We'll* be a monument of sorts,"
my father says,
"a part of what they fought for
long ago."

"Maybe they know," I say.

I lift a piece of gravel
that is lying
close to where the builders dug.
It's shaped just like a pigeon's egg,
more pointed, flattened on one side.
Is it a bullet?
A hundred years and more it's lain here.
I'll keep it for a souvenir.

No.

I weigh it in my hand,
then throw it high
across the field of bones.

How silently it falls
into the tufts of grass
and flowers.

The resting birds
rise up together,
fly.
I see their wings,
the blue and gray,
against the shine of sky.

Suggestions for Further Reading

PICTURE BOOKS

ACKERMAN, KAREN, *Tin Heart* (illus. by MICHAEL HAYS), New York: Atheneum, 1990.

LYON, GEORGE ELLA, *Cecil's Story* (illus. by PETER CATALANOTTO), New York: Orchard Books, 1991.

POLACCO, PATRICIA, *Pink and Say,* New York: Philomel Books, 1994.

TURNER, ANN, *Nettie's Trip South* (illus. by RONALD HIMLER), New York: Simon & Schuster, 1987.

WINTER, JEANETTE, *Follow the Drinking Gourd,* New York: Dragonfly Books/Knopf, 1988.

NONFICTION

FRITZ, JEAN, *Just a Few Words, Mr. Lincoln: The Story of the Gettysburg Address* (illus. by CHARLES ROBINSON), New York: Putnam, 1993.

LEVINE, ELLEN, *. . . If You Traveled on the Underground Railroad* (illus. by LARRY JOHNSON), New York: Scholastic Inc., 1993.

MOORE, KAY, *. . . If You Lived at the Time of the Civil War* (illus. by ANNI MATSICK), New York: Scholastic Inc., 1994.

MURPHY, JIM, *The Boys' War,* New York: Clarion Books, 1990.

POETRY

GREENFIELD, ELOISE, "Harriet Tubman," from *Honey, I Love: And Other Love Poems* (illus. by LEO AND DIANE DILLON), New York: HarperCollins, 1978.

To my friends Dolly and Mel
and to Tony Bear, who gave me that gift
— E.B.

To Dianne Hess, for taking a chance on me
— N.B.

Library of Congress Cataloging-in-Publication Data
Bunting, Eve, 1928-
  The blue and the gray / by Eve Bunting; illustrated by Ned Bittinger.
    p.   cm.
  Summary: As a black boy and his white friend watch the construction
of a house which will make them neighbors on the site of a Civil War
battlefield, they agree that their homes are monuments to that war.
  ISBN 0-590-60197-0
  1. United States — History — Civil War, 1861-1865 — Juvenile fiction.
[1. United States — History — Civil War, 1861-1865 — Fiction.
2. Friendship — Fiction. 3. Dwellings — Fiction. 4. Afro-Americans — Fiction.
5. Stories in rhyme.] I. Bittinger, Ned, ill. II. Title.
PZ8.3.B92B1   1996
[E] — dc20   95-30902
CIP
AC
12 11 10 9 8 7 6 5 4 3 2 1   6 7 8 9/9 0 1/0
Printed in Singapore   46
First printing, November 1996

The display type was set in Pelican from Adobe.
The text type was set in Clearface by WLCR New York.
Ned Bittinger's art was rendered in oils on primed linen.

Special thanks to The Civil War Society, Berryville, Virginia,
for fact-checking the manuscript and the art.